提姆·波頓 ● 悲慘故事集

牡蠣男孩
憂鬱之死

提姆·波頓 著

林則良——譯

The Melancholy Death of
OYSTER BOY
and
Other Stories

Tim Burton

獻給麗莎・瑪莉
For Lisa Marie

目錄 | Contents |

熱戀中的枯枝男孩
和火柴女郎

枯枝男孩喜歡火柴女郎，
他對她十分中意，
他喜歡她俏麗身影，
他覺得她火辣熱情。

Stick Boy and
Match Girl in Love

Stick Boy liked Match Girl,
He liked her a lot.
He liked her cute figure,
he thought she was hot.

不過愛火可曾，
為枯枝和火柴燃起？
當然那愛火一發不可收拾，
他轉眼燒個不停。

But could a flame ever burn
for a match and a stick?
It did quite literally;
he burned up pretty quick.

機器人男孩

史密斯太太和史密斯先生美滿幸福，
他們是很平凡很快樂的妻子和丈夫。
一天他們得知讓史密斯先生歡天喜地的好消息。
史密斯太太要當媽了，
所以他就要做爸了！
然而他們的喜悅結晶卻出了點兒岔，
它怎麼看怎麼不像個人，
它是個機器娃兒！

Robot Boy

Mr. and Mrs. Smith had a wonderful life.
They were a normal, happy husband and wife.
One day they got news that made Mr. Smith glad.
Mrs. Smith would be a mom,
which would make him the dad!
But something was wrong with their bundle of joy.
It wasn't human at all,
it was a robot boy!

他既沒溫度也不惹人疼，
他甚至沒膚又沒皮，
除了冷冰冰、薄怯怯的一層錫，
還有那頭上伸出的管子和電線。
他躺在那兒目不轉睛，
非死亦非生。

唯有接上延長線、
插入牆上的電插頭，
那一刻他才顯得靈氣活現。

He wasn't warm and cuddly
and he didn't have skin.
Instead, there was a cold, thin layer of tin.
There were wires and tubes sticking out of his head.
He just lay there and stared,
not living or dead.

The only time he seemed alive at all
was with a long extension cord
plugged into the wall.

史密斯先生對著醫生吼吼叫叫：
「你到底對我兒子動了什麼手腳？
他沒血也沒肉，
是個鋁合金怪獸！」

Mr. Smith yelled at the doctor,
"What have you done to my boy?
He's not flesh and blood,
he's aluminum alloy!"

醫生回以輕聲細語：
「我接下來要告訴你的事，
聽起來實在難以置信。
不過你並非是，
這怪小孩的親生父親。
你看，連小孩到底是男是女，
到現在依舊撲朔迷離，
不過我們認為孩子的親生父親，
是一只微波攪拌機。」

The doctor said gently,
"What I'm going to say
will sound pretty wild.
But you're not the father
of this strange-looking child.
You see, there still is some question
about the child's gender,
but we think that its father
is a microwave blender."

從此史密斯家的生活，
雪上加霜且雞犬不寧。
史密斯太太恨他老公，
他則恨他老婆。
他永遠無法原諒，
老婆背著他暗地私通，
而對象竟然會是——
廚房的一台電器。

如今機器人男孩，
已長成一位年輕男子。
雖然他老被人錯認為——
是垃圾箱一只。

The Smiths' lives were now filled
with misery and strife.
Mrs. Smith hated her husband,
and he hated his wife.
He never forgave her unholy alliance:
a sexual encounter
with a kitchen appliance.

And Robot Boy
grew to be a young man.
Though he was often mistaken
for a garbage can.

瞪大眼女孩

我認識那麼一個女孩，
光站在那裡瞪大雙眼。
不管看東還是看西，
她一點兒都不在意。

Staring Girl

I once knew a girl
who would just stand there and stare.
At anyone or anything,
she seemed not to care.

她會對地面瞪大眼，

She'd stare at the ground,

21

她會對天空瞪大眼。

She'd stare at the sky.

她會瞪你瞪好幾個小時，
而你還是一頭霧水。

She'd stare at you for hours,
and you'd never know why.

不過自從她榮獲本地的瞪眼冠軍，

But after winning the local staring contest,

她那雙大眼最後終於
贏得最妥善的休息。

she finally gave her eyes
a well-deserved rest.

眼中釘男孩

雙眼釘了鐵釘的男孩，
在擺設他那棵鋁樹。
樹的模樣看來真滑稽，
那全是他霧裡看花的緣故。

The Boy with Nails
in His Eyes

The Boy with Nails in His Eyes
put up his aluminum tree.
It looked pretty strange
because he couldn't really see.

臉上都是眼睛
的女孩

那天人在公園，
我非常非常吃驚；
我遇到一個女孩，
臉上都是眼睛。

The Girl
with Many Eyes

One day in the park
I had quite a surprise.
I met a girl
who had many eyes.

她人長得真是漂亮，
（而且還真嚇人一跳！）
我注意到她有張櫻桃小嘴，
所以我們開始東聊西聊。

我們聊她課堂念的詩，
我們談及鮮花朵朵，
我們還聊到若她得戴眼鏡，
那可真會麻煩多多。

She was really quite pretty
(and also quite shocking!)
and I noticed she had a mouth,
so we ended up talking.

We talked about flowers,
and her poetry classes,
and the problems she'd have
if she ever wore glasses.

能遇見一個女孩
滿臉都是眼睛，
這實在叫人開心。
不過要是她落淚傷心，
你就會變成一隻落湯雞。

It's great to know a girl
who has so many eyes,
but you really get wet
when she breaks down and cries.

污漬小子傳奇

所有的超級英雄裡，
就屬他最怪異，
他不開時髦跑車，
也沒半點超自然力。

若和超人蝙蝠俠相比，
我想他算安分守己，
不過我覺得他真神奇，
污漬小子就是他英名。

Stain Boy

Of all the super heroes,
the strangest one by far,
doesn't have a special power,
or drive a fancy car.

Next to Superman and Batman,
I guess he must seem tame.
But to me he is quite special,
and Stain Boy is his name.

他沒辦法繞著高樓大廈飛，
也沒辦法跑得比高速火車快；
但說到留下髒兮兮的污漬，
這傢伙可是蓋世天才。

He can't fly around tall buildings,
or outrun a speeding train,
the only talent he seems to have
is to leave a nasty stain.

我知道他有時也傷透腦筋，
既不會飛不會游也不會跑，
況且正因他唯一的超能力，
他送乾洗的帳單堆得比天還高。

Sometimes I know it bothers him,
that he can't run or swim or fly,
and because of this one ability,
his dry cleaning bill's sky-high.

牡蠣男孩憂鬱之死

The Melancholy Death of Oyster Boy

他在沙丘上求婚，

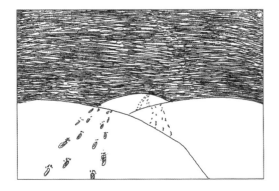

He proposed in the dunes,

他們在海邊成親。

they were wed by the sea,

在卡普利島，他們慶祝
為期九天的蜜月旅行。

their nine-day-long honeymoon
was on the isle of Capri.

晚餐他們點了一客特大號、
一鍋全是淡菜和魚的燉湯。
當他品嘗那鍋海鮮，
做新娘的她默默許下心願。

For their supper they had one spectacular dish—
a simmering stew of mollusks and fish.
And while he savored the broth,
her bride's heart made a wish.

心願成真──她生下一個小娃。
不過這小傢伙可有半點人樣？
好吧，
約莫七七八八。

十隻手指十隻腳趾，
他會消化會看東西。
他會聽，他有感應，
但一切正常？
說來未必。
這非自然的生命，這禍害，這病源，
是他們一切苦難的起始與終結。

That wish did come true—she gave birth to a baby.
But was this little one human?
Well,
maybe.

Ten fingers, ten toes,
he had plumbing and sight.
He could hear, he could feel,
but normal?
Not quite.
This unnatural birth, this canker, this blight,
was the start and the end and the sum of their plight.

她對著大夫埋怨：
「他不可能是我親生骨肉。
他渾身都是海洋、水草和鹽水的味道。」

She railed at the doctor:
"He cannot be mine.
He smells of the ocean, of seaweed and brine."

「你已該感到慶幸，不過就在上個星期，
我還治療過一個女孩，有著三只耳朵和一張鳥喙。
你兒子生來有一半是牡蠣，
這不能歸罪於我。
……倒要問問你有沒有閃過這樣的念頭，
不如舉家搬遷到海灘上頭？」

"You should count yourself lucky, for only last week,
I treated a girl with three ears and a beak.
That your son is half oyster
you cannot blame me.
...have you considered, by chance,
a small home by the sea?"

不知該如何取名，
他們隨口叫他山姆，
或者，偶爾也叫他──
「那個看起來像蛤蜊的東西。」

每個人都在揣測但無人知曉，
小山姆何時會脫殼而出？

Not knowing what to name him,
they just called him Sam,
or, sometimes,
"that thing that looks like a clam."

Everyone wondered, but no one could tell,
When would young Oyster Boy come out of his shell?

一天湯普生家的四胞胎在外偷看，
他們喊他「蚵仔！」然後一哄而散。

When the Thompson quadruplets espied him one day,
they called him a bivalve and ran quickly away.

某個春日午後，
山姆被遺棄在滂沱雨中，
在海景街和主街交口的西南角落，
他凝望著雨水打轉然後
看它們一路流進排水溝。

One spring afternoon,
Sam was left in the rain.
At the southwestern corner of Seaview and Main,
he watched the rain water as it swirled
down the drain.

他母親人在高速公路
交通癱瘓的線道上頭，
她猛拍汽車儀表板——
她無法承受
不斷在心頭翻騰的悲慟、
沮喪、
和苦痛。

His mom on the freeway
in the breakdown lane
was pounding the dashboard—
she couldn't contain
the ever-rising grief,
frustration,
and pain.

「說真的，甜心」她說：
「我可不是在說笑，
但我一直聞到魚腥味，
我想那來自咱們的寶貝。
我不想說但我必須說，
你不能把自己的不舉，全推給咱們生的那小傢伙。」

他敷軟膏，他塗藥膏，
結果全身紅腫。
他試春藥，他用乳液，
他又吃酊劑來力圖振作。
結果他又痛又癢又抽搐又流血。

"Really, sweetheart," she said,
"I don't mean to make fun,
but something smells fishy
and I think it's our son.
I don't like to say this, but it must be said,
you're blaming our son for your problems in bed."

He tried salves, he tried ointments
that turned everything red.
He tried potions and lotions
and tincture of lead.
He ached and he itched and he twitched and he bled.

根據大夫診斷：
「我不敢百分百確定，
但問題之所在可能就是解藥之所在。
據說牡蠣可以增進雄風，
也許把你兒子吃下肚裡，
能讓你好好幹活數小時不停。」

The doctor diagnosed,
"I can't be quite sure,
but the cause of the problem may also be the cure.
They say oysters improve your sexual powers.
Perhaps eating your son
would help you do it for hours!"

他躡手躡腳，
他偷偷走近，
他額頭冒著汗，
他嘴唇——在說謊。
「兒子呀，你快樂嗎？我不是有意打探，
不過你是否嚮往天國？
你是否想過一死百了？」

He came on tiptoe,
he came on the sly,
sweat on his forehead,
and on his lips—a lie.
"Son, are you happy? I don't mean to pry,
but do you dream of Heaven?
Have you wanted to die?"

山姆眨了兩次眼，
不說一句話。
老爸握了握菜刀，而後鬆了鬆領帶。

Sam blinked his eyes twice.
but made no reply.
Dad fingered his knife and loosened his tie.

當他舉起自己的兒子，
山姆滴了汁在他大衣上頭。
他把殼靠在唇上，
山姆便沿著他喉嚨滑落。

As he picked up his son,
Sam dripped on his coat.
With the shell to his lips,
Sam slipped down his throat.

他們在海邊的沙地草草埋了他
——念一段禱詞，滴一滴眼淚——
下午三點就回到了家。

牡蠣男孩墓上插著灰白的浮木十字架。
他的墓誌銘寫在沙上，
允諾他重回天父的懷抱。

They buried him quickly in the sand by the sea
—sighed a prayer, wept a tear—
and were back home by three.

A cross of gray driftwood marked Oyster Boy's grave.
Words writ in the sand
promised Jesus would save.

不過一陣漲潮，就使他一生的記憶隨波漂逝。

But his memory was lost with one high-tide wave.

回到家安心躺臥在床，
他親吻她然後說：
「我們來吧。」

Back home safe in bed,
he kissed her and said,
"Let's give it a whirl."

「但這一次，」她輕聲細語：
「願我們生的是個女娃。」

"But this time," she whispered, "we'll wish for a girl."

巫毒女郎

她的肌膚是一襲白布，
她的全身縫縫補補，
還有一堆彩色大頭針，
從她的心臟裡頭刺出。

她有一雙漂亮、
不斷環繞旋轉的電眼，
一雙能夠妖惑催眠、
眾家魯男子的媚眼。

Voodoo Girl

Her skin is white cloth,
and she's all sewn apart
and she has many colored pins
sticking out of her heart.

She has a beautiful set
of hypno-disk eyes,
the ones that she uses
to hypnotize guys.

各式各樣的殭屍，
對她深深著魔。
她甚至網羅了殭屍一隻，
遠道來自法國。

She has many different zombies
who are deeply in her trance.
She even has a zombie
who was originally from France.

不過她知道自己深受詛咒，
這躲也躲不掉的厄運。
一旦哪個人
想進一步接近，

那些彩色大頭針就愈刺愈進去。

But she knows she has a curse on her,
a curse she cannot win.
For if someone gets
too close to her,

the pins stick farther in.

污漬小子別開生面
的耶誕節

耶誕佳節，污漬小子收到一件新制服，
潔白乾爽燙得整整齊齊，
暖和又舒服。

Stain Boy's
Special Christmas

For Christmas, Stain Boy got a new uniform.
It was clean and well pressed,
comfy and warm.

但不消幾分鐘，
（絕不超過十分鐘）

―――――――――――――――――――

But in a few short minutes,
(no longer than ten)

溼漉漉、油膩膩的污漬，
又全身皆是。

those wet, greasy stains
started forming again.

化作一張眠床
的女孩

自從那一天，
她摘下某種稀奇的貓柳，
她的頭顱就開始鼓脹發白，
輕柔，一如枕頭。

她的肌膚，已轉變，
層層疊疊，且質變，
現在已改頭換面，
呈百分百純棉。

The Girl
Who Turned into a Bed

It happened that day
she picked some strange pussy willow.
Her head swelled up white
and soft as a pillow.

Her skin, which had turned
all flaky and rotten,
was now replaced
with 100% cotton.

而她身上的器官和軀幹，
已生成羽翼的模樣，
長成漂亮的擺設，
由床墊和彈簧構成。

Through her organs and torso
she sprouted like wings,
a beautiful set
of mattress and springs.

這實在怪異得叫人膽戰心驚，
我為此開始啜泣。
不過哭過之後至少，
我有個好去處能一覺到天明。

It was so terribly strange
that I started to weep.
But at least after that
I had a nice place to sleep.

羅伊，那個劇毒男孩

我們這群認識他的人
──他的親朋──
都管他叫羅伊。
對其他不認識他的人，
他則是「那個可怕的劇毒男孩」。

Roy, the Toxic Boy

To those of us who knew him
—his friends—
we called him Roy.
To others he was known
as that horrible Toxic Boy.

他熱愛阿摩尼亞和石棉，
他還酷愛大量二手煙。
他所賴以維生的空氣，
會讓大多數人缺氧窒息！

他最愛的小玩具，
是一小罐噴霧器；
他可以一整天不吵不鬧坐在那裡，
三不五時就搖搖噴噴那罐噴霧器。

He loved ammonia and asbestos,
and lots of cigarette smoke.
What he breathed in for air
would make most people choke!

His very favorite toy
was a can of aerosol spray;
he'd sit quietly and shake it,
and spray it all the day.

在天寒地凍的清晨，
他會站在車庫裡，
靜待車子起火發動，
好讓自己沉浸引擎廢氣之中。

He'd stand inside of the garage
in the early-morning frost,
waiting for the car to start
and fill him with exhaust.

絕無僅有獨此一回，
我親眼目睹劇毒男孩淚眼汪汪。
只因當時有食鹽少許，
恰巧落入他的眼眶。

The one and only time
I ever saw Toxic Boy cry
was when some sodium chloride
got into his eye.

有天為了呼吸新鮮空氣，
他們把他安置在花園裡。

他的臉色頓時慘白，
他的身體開始僵硬。

One day for fresh air
they put him in the garden.

His face went deathly pale
and his body began to harden.

在他短暫一生的彌留之際，
他病態焉焉絕望至極。
誰會想到呼吸戶外空氣，
竟會致人於絕境死地？

The final gasp of his short life
was sickly with despair.
Whoever thought that you could die
from breathing outdoor air?

當羅伊的靈魂脫離身軀，
我們全體為他默哀致敬。
他的靈魂直上天際，
徒留破洞在臭氧層裡。

As Roy's soul left his body,
we all said a silent prayer.
It drifted up to heaven
and left a hole in the ozone layer.

詹姆斯

真不高明，耶誕老公公給了詹姆斯一隻泰迪熊當禮物，萬萬沒想到他早些時候，才被一隻大灰熊撕扯得體無完膚。

James

Unwisely, Santa offered a teddy bear to James, unaware that he had been mauled by a grizzly earlier that year.

枯枝男孩的
耶誕季節

枯枝男孩發現他的耶誕樹怎麼看
都比他健壯。

Stick Boy's Festive Season

Stick Boy noticed that his Christmas tree looked
healthier than he did.

布利起司小子

布利起司小子有兩次夢見，
他渾圓的大頭只剩一小片。

Brie Boy

Brie Boy had a dream he only had twice,
that his full, round head was only a slice.

其他小孩都不肯和布利起司小子一起玩……
……但他至少和優質夏多內[1]是天生絕配。

The other children never let Brie Boy play...
...but at least he went well with a nice Chardonnay.

木乃伊男孩

他沒有軟香粉嫩的肌膚，
也沒有圓滾滾的小肥肚；
他裡面空空外殼堅硬，
他是個小男孩木乃伊。

「醫生，拜託行行好，
告訴我們到底是誰造的孽？
為何我們的一場歡快，
卻換來這破布一團？」

Mummy Boy

He wasn't soft and pink
with a fat little tummy;
he was hard and hollow,
a little boy mummy.

"Tell us, please, Doctor,
the reason or cause,
why our bundle of joy
is just a bundle of gauze."

「我的診斷是，」他說，
「姑且不論是好是壞，
你們的兒子是遭到了
古法老王詛咒的遺害。」

"My diagnosis," he said,
"for better or worse,
is that your son is the result
of an old pharaoh's curse."

當天晚上他們談了又談，
他們兒子離奇古怪的處境。
他們管他叫：「一件
被考古探險隊遺棄的次級品」。

他們緊抓腦袋尋思，
那些複雜的科學解釋，
但最終假設那只不過是，
超自然的投胎轉世。

That night they talked
of their son's odd condition—
they called him "a reject
from an archaeological expedition."

They thought of some complex
scientific explanation,
but assumed it was simple
supernatural reincarnation.

和其他的幼齒小娃娃，
他只一起玩過兩次
古代處女獻祭的遊戲。
（不過娃娃們全都嚇跑，嚷著：
「你真不是個好東西！」）

With the other young tots
he only played twice,
an ancient game of virgin sacrifice.
(But the kids ran away, saying, "You aren't very nice.")

孤獨一人飽受嫌棄，木乃伊男孩暗自落淚，
然後他走向儲藏櫃，
那裡擺著好吃的零嘴。

Alone and rejected, Mummy Boy wept,
then went to the cabinet
where the snack food was kept.

他用木乃伊屍布的衣袖拭去淚溼的眼窩，
倒了一碗沾滿糖霜的唐納葉[1]入座。

He wiped his wet sockets with his mummified sleeves,
and sat down to a bowl of sugar-frosted tanna leaves.

107

一天天色晦暗而陰森，
霧茫茫之中，
跑出一隻蒼白的木乃伊小狗。

One dark, gloomy day,
from out of the fog,
appeared a little white mummy dog.

為了這新撿到的繃帶寵物，
他著實費了不少工夫，
他還為牠蓋了一間
仿照埃及金字塔的狗屋。

For his newfound wrapped pet,
he did many things,
like building a dog house
à la Pyramid of Kings.

一天時候已晚，
轉眼天就要黑了。
木乃伊男孩牽著狗，
來到公園散散步。

It was late in the day—
just before dark.
Mummy Boy took his dog
for a walk in the park.

公園裡冷冷清清，
觸目所及只有一隻松鼠，
還有一個墨西哥女孩的生日派對。

男孩女孩玩得正開心，
卻留意到那個像紙漿糊出來的玩意。

The park was empty
except for a squirrel,
and a birthday party for a Mexican girl.

The boys and girls had all started to play,
but noticed that thing that looked like papier mâché.

「你看，是個皮納塔[2]，」
其中一個男孩說：
「我們快把它敲開來，
裡面會有玩具和糖果。」

他們拿了一支球棒，
朝他的大頭猛擊。
木乃伊男孩不支倒地，
最後終於當場斃命。

"Look, it's a piñata,"
said one of the boys,
"let's crack it wide open
and get the candy and toys."

They took a baseball bat
and whacked open his head.
Mummy Boy fell to the ground;
he finally was dead.

在他的大頭殼裡，
既沒糖果也沒獎品，
只有幾隻迷路的甲蟲，
大大小小不一。

Inside of his head
were no candy or prizes,
just a few stray beetles
of various sizes.

拉箕女孩

從前從前有個女孩，
她整個人就是拉箕。
她怎麼看怎麼骯髒，
怎麼聞怎麼像臭鼬。

她總是悶悶不樂，
三不五時陷入低潮——這或許就是因為，
她花太多時間混垃圾堆。

Junk Girl

There once was a girl
who was made up of junk.
She looked really dirty,
and she smelled like a skunk.

She was always unhappy,
or in one of her slumps—perhaps 'cause she spent
so much time down in the dumps.

她唯一開朗的時刻，
全仰賴一位名叫史丹的傢伙。
他就住附近，
他專撿垃圾。

The only bright moment
was from a guy named Stan.
He was the neighborhood
garbage man.

他很愛她，
而且還跟她求了親，
只不過她早將自己，
許給了垃圾輾碎機。

He loved her a lot
and made a marriage proposal,
but she'd already thrown herself
down a garbage disposal.

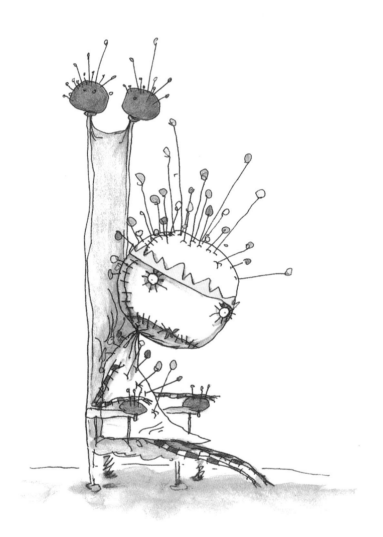

針插女王

對針插女王來說，
日子真的難過，
她一坐上王位寶座，
針就穿脾而過。

The Pin Cushion Queen

Life isn't easy
for the Pin Cushion Queen.
When she sits on her throne
pins push through her spleen.

香瓜大頭

從前有個憂鬱的香瓜大頭，
終日坐在那邊，
一心只想早日離開人間。

Melonhead

There once was a morose melonhead,
who sat there all day
and wished he were dead.

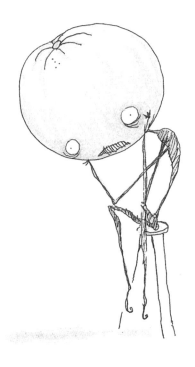

不過你得當心，
不要隨便許願。
因為他聽見的最後一聲，
是震耳欲聾的踩碎瓜聲。

But you should be careful
about the things that you wish.
Because the last thing he heard
was a deafening squish.

蘇

為了避免法律告訴，
我們姑且叫她蘇，
（不然就叫「那個女孩愛把膠
吸得唏哩呼嚕」）。

Sue

To avoid a lawsuit,
we'll just call her Sue
(or "that girl who likes
to sniff lots of glue").

我之所以敢斷言
她有這般惡習，
全在她一擤鼻涕，

The reason I know
that this is the case
is when she blows her nose,

舒潔就黏上臉去。

---

kleenex sticks to her face.

吉米，那個醜不拉嘰的
企鵝男孩

「我叫吉米，
不過我朋友都只管叫我：
『那個醜不拉嘰的企鵝男孩。』」

Jimmy, the Hideous
Penguin Boy

"My name is Jimmy,
but my friends just call me
'the hideous penguin boy.'"

焦炭男孩

耶誕佳節，
焦炭男孩一如往常收到一小塊煤當禮物，
讓他非常開心。

Char Boy

For Christmas,
Char Boy received his usual lump of coal,
which made him very happy.

耶誕佳節，
焦炭男孩收到一件小玩意，
不如往常是一小塊煤，
這讓他百思不解。

For Christmas,
Char Boy received a small present instead of
his usual lump of coal,
which confused him very much.

耶誕佳節，
焦炭男孩被誤以為是一堆髒兮兮的煤灰，
被一把掃到大街上去。

For Christmas,
Char Boy was mistaken for a dirty fireplace
and swept out into the street.

錨兒

曾經有那麼一個女孩，
她來自蔚藍大海。
而只有那麼一個地方，
她一心深深嚮往。

為了一個名叫沃克的男子，
那個在樂團裡彈唱的男子。
她離開大海，
投奔陸地異鄉。

Anchor Baby

There was a beautiful girl
who came from the sea.
And there was just one place
that she wanted to be.

With a man named Walker
who played in a band.
She would leave the ocean
and come onto the land.

他是她唯一、
她唯一的心之所欲。
她費盡一切心機，
欲擄獲他神出鬼沒的魅影。

然而他們的生命境遇，
卻始終毫無交集。
她在陸上千迴百折，
獨自一人四處碰壁。

He was the one
that she wanted the most.
And she tried everything
to capture this ghost.

But throughout all their lives
they never connected.
She wandered the earth
alone and rejected.

她讓自己看起來開心，
她讓自己看起來悲戚，
她嘗試靈體飛行，
也試過性愛和邪靈附體。

什麼也無法讓他們結合，
除非一樣東西也許……
只是也許……
能將他們的靈魂以錨固定
——他們有了小貝比。

_____

She tried looking happy
she tried looking tragic,
she tried astral projecting,
sex, and black magic.

Nothing could join them,
except maybe one thing,
just maybe...
something to anchor their spirits....
They had a baby.

但是為了生出小貝比，
他們得動用一台起重機。
銜接嬰兒的那條臍帶，
看來就是鐵鍊無疑。

它又醜又黑，
而且硬得像鐵茶壺。
它沒有粉嫩的肌膚，
只有沉重鉛灰的金屬。

But to give birth to the baby
they needed a crane.
The umbilical cord
was in the form of a chain.

It was ugly and gloomy,
and as hard as a kettle.
It had no pink skin,
just heavy gray metal.

小嬰兒原本生來，
該讓他倆廝守一起，
現在卻讓他們，
籠罩在淒風苦雨的陰霾裡。

The baby that was meant
to bring them together,
just shrouded them both
in a cloud of foul weather.

於是沃克趁機開溜，
跑回樂團彈彈唱唱。
就從那一天起，
他幾乎只待在陸上。

留下她隻身一人，
和她鉛灰的錨兒；
一切如此難過沉悶，
終究讓她直往下沉。

So Walker took off
to play with the band.
And from that day on,
he stayed mainly on land.

And she was alone
with her gray baby anchor,
who got so oppressive
that it eventually sank her.

當她沉到海底深處，
她的願望已成泡沫，
唯獨她、她的錨兒……
和幾隻稀稀落落的魚兒。

As she went to the bottom,
not fulfilling her wish,
it was her, and her baby...
and a few scattered fish.

牡蠣男孩出門去

迎接萬聖節，
牡蠣男孩決心像其他人一樣歡度佳節。

Oyster Boy Steps Out

For Halloween,
Oyster Boy decided to go as a human.

| Acknowledgments |

感謝
Michael McDowell, Jill Jacobs Brack,
Rodney Kizziah, Eva Quiroz
以及
David Szanto

Fluffy FZI0110

提姆‧波頓悲慘故事集（問世20週年紀念版）──

牡蠣男孩憂鬱之死
The Melancholy Death of Oyster Boy and Other Stories

作　　者─提姆‧波頓 Tim Burton
譯　　者─林則良
主　　編─CHIENWEI WANG
封面設計─廖　韡
內頁設計─山今工作室
執行企劃─劉凱瑛

總 編 輯─余宜芳
董 事 長─趙政岷
出 版 者─時報文化出版企業股份有限公司
　　　　　108019台北市和平西路三段240號3樓
　　　　　發行專線─（02）23066842
　　　　　讀者服務專線─0800231705‧（02）23047103
　　　　　讀者服務傳真─（02）23046858
　　　　　郵撥─19344724 時報文化出版公司
　　　　　信箱─10899臺北華江橋郵局第99信箱
時報悅讀網─www.readingtimes.com.tw
法律顧問─理律法律事務所陳長文律師、李念祖律師
印　　刷─和楹印刷有限公司
初版一刷─2009年7月06日
二版十刷─2023年11月06日
定　　價─新台幣280元

ISBN 978-957-13-6717-0
Printed in Taiwan

牡蠣男孩憂鬱之死：提姆・波頓悲慘故事集
（問世20週年紀念版）/
提姆・波頓著；林則良譯. -- 初版.
-- 臺北市：時報文化, 2016.08
152面；13x20.4 公分. --（Fluffy 叢書；FZI0110）
譯自：The Melancholy Death of Oyster Boy & Other Stories
ISBN 978-957-13-6717-0（平裝）

1.美國文學　　　2.繪本

874.6　　　　　　　　　　　　　　105011432